MW00953910

DINO TREASURES

by Rhonda Lucas Donald
illustrated by Cathy Morrison

NESTING

The tiny dino eggs lie in a cozy nest.
They're safe and warm tucked under momma's breast.
In a little while the eggs begin to hatch.
And momma brings to eat whatever she can catch.

Other fossils show that dad was caring too.
While mom went to eat, dad warmed the growing brood
Raising baby dinos took a lot of care.
It's easier to do when working as a pair.

SKIN SAMPLES

Say, can you describe what dino skin was like?
If you said, "it's scaly," you'd be in the right.
But finding dino skin is not an easy task.
Most fossils are of bone, as skin just doesn't last.

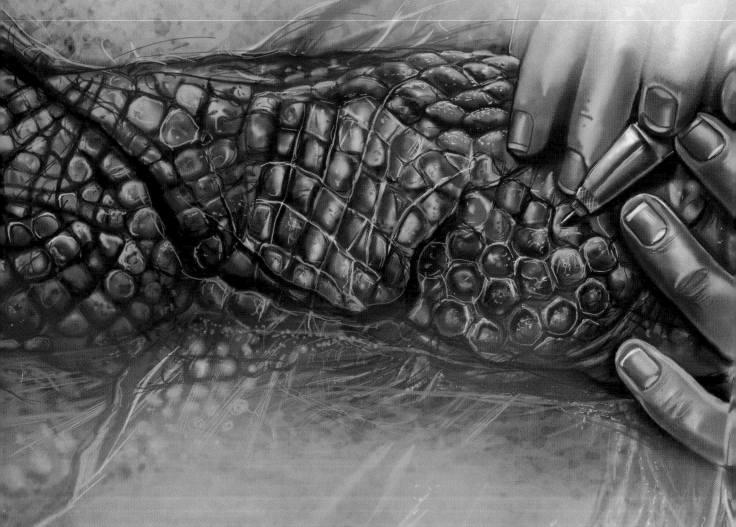

Can you now imagine how great it must have been
to find a duckbill fossil complete with dino skin?
Plain as you can see are scales of different size,
which makes this fossil find a rare and special prize.

FEATHERS

Everybody knows that feathers are for birds.
But dinos had them too, in case you hadn't heard.
Some were kind of fuzzy and others fully plumed.
Many more had feathers than anyone assumed.

So what's with all the feathers? Could the dinos fly?
Maybe they helped keep a dino warm and dry.
Or they might have helped to show off to a mate.
That's the way a peacock tries to get a date!

COLORFUL CRITTERS

A fossil doesn't come in color that is true.
Even though it's rock, it still may hold a clue.
Fossils showing feathers have a tale to tell.
So if you look inside them, you will know as well.

Tiny little shapes, too small for you to see,
tell a feather's tale and the color it would be.
Magnify the shapes and then you have the news:
lots of dino feathers came in many hues.

DINO POOP

Did you know that dino poop's a fossil too?
You can learn a lot when you look at dino doo.
Some have bits of bone, teeth—even fishy scales.
These all came from meat-eating dinos without fail.

Other samples show remains of plants and leaves.
Veggie-saurus left them behind, we do believe.
Even more amazing are tunnels in the poo,
left behind by beetles that fed on dung—it's true!

WHAT'S FOR DINNER?

What a dino ate is hard to know for sure.
Teeth provide a clue, and poop does even more!
But some fossils show a dino's final meal,
the proof is in the tum and what it can reveal.

Some dinos dined on others smaller than they were.
Some munched on birds, eating feathers and not fur.
One had a meal leaving teeth and scales from fish.
Another fed on plants, no doubt its favorite dish!

WHAT DID DINOS SOUND LIKE?

This duckbilled dinosaur had a crest for all to see.
But what the crest was for is quite a mystery.
Was it a fighting weapon or super-sniffing tool?
Was it a fashion statement to make a dino cool?

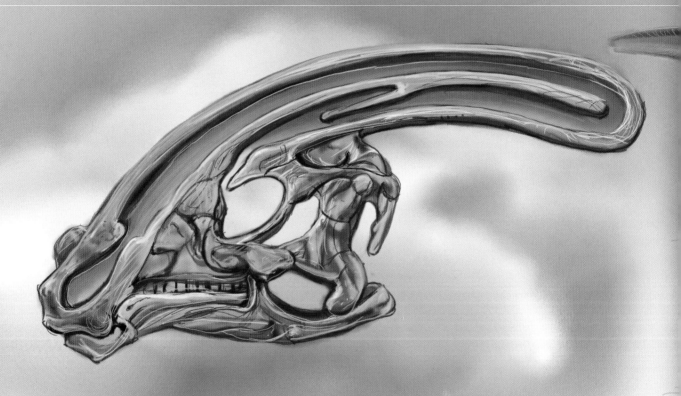

So a team decided to peek inside the crest.
Seems the crest was hollow—who could ever guess?
When they tried to copy what kind of sound it made,
they heard a rumbling call the dino could have brayed.

TOUGH LIFE

Living in the wild is dangerous and rough.
Dinos must have thrived by being pretty tough.
Proof that life was hard is written in the bone.
Scars, tooth marks, and illness are positively shown.

Sue, the mighty *T. rex*, is just one case in point.
She had broken ribs, injured limbs, and painful joints.
Poor old injured Sue had pain, it's safe to say.
It proves that life was hard for predator and prey.

FIGHTING DINOS

Hunting, chasing dinos looked out for a meal.
They would eat whatever they could catch or steal.
Dinos being chased weren't easy to defeat.
Spiky horns and armor made them tough to beat.

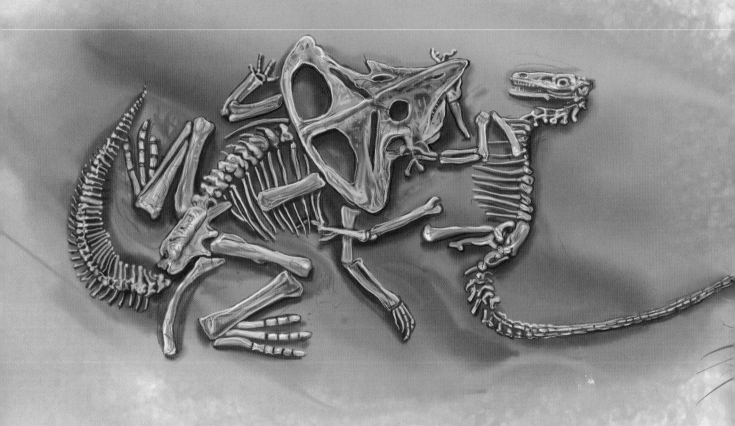

When the two would meet, oh what a mighty fight.
One amazing fossil shows us all the sight.
There, in solid rock, dinos battle for their lives.
Caught in shifting sand, though, neither one survived.

SLEEPING

In an ancient forest among volcanic domes,
lived a tiny dino to which the place was home.
What her life was like, we cannot know—it's true.
We know the way she slept because we have a clue.

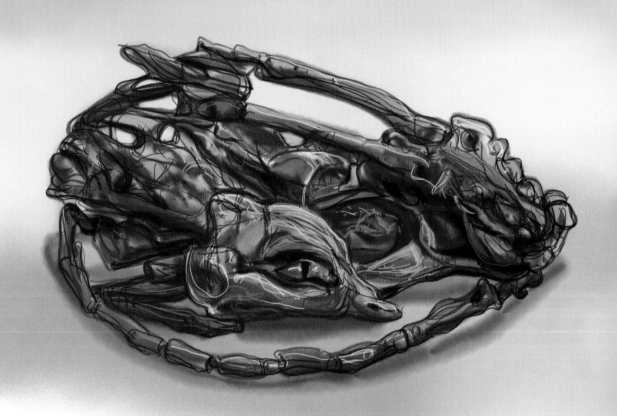

Curled up in a ball the sleeping dino lay.
"What's the deal with that?" you very well may say.
Look, her head is tucked up 'neath her little wing.
She slept like birds today—now isn't that the thing?

TRACKS

When you think of fossils, you may think of bones.
There are other traces left behind in stone.
Some of these are footprints that dinos left behind.
Follow in their footsteps and see what you can find.

The tracks can show how slow or fast a dino moved.
Did it walk on four feet or get along on two?
Some walked all alone and others in a herd.
You can even learn what food the beast preferred.

HEAD BUTTING DINOS

Two bighorn sheep go charging on a mountainside,
running toward each other 'til they both collide.
When the two butt heads you hear a mighty crack!
Rams fight off their rivals with horns that take a whack.

Helmet-headed dinos might have done the same.
Butting thick-skulled heads was not an easy game.
Fossils show the skulls had injuries and breaks.
Seems that butting heads would lead to bad headaches!

BIRDS ARE DINOSAURS

Are you sad to think that dinosaurs are gone?
Would you like to know they really do live on?
Look outside your window or in the nearest tree—
dinosaurs are there as plain as you can see.

No more do giants walk with steps to shake the ground
No longer to the land are many of them bound.
But they still have feathers, and so in other words,
dinosaurs aren't gone; they live on in the birds!

For Creative Minds

Biologist or Paleontologist?

Scientists who study living things (biologists) often observe animals to learn about them. If they are working in the field, they might even see different animal signs (nests with eggs, footprints, or poop) that help them to better understand the animal they are studying.

Scientists who study dinosaurs (paleontologists) learn about the animals by studying body or trace fossil clues. They sometimes use knowledge of today's animals to help them understand the dinosaurs.

Identify whether you think the following statements describe the work of a biologist or a paleontologist. Can you explain "why" to someone?

1. The scientist dissected the owl pellet to see what it had eaten.

2. The scientist discovered that the round-looking rock was fossilized poop (coprolite) containing bits of bone from a plant-eating dinosaur.

3. In 2011, scientists found several dinosaur feathers trapped in amber.

4. In 2007, scientists found a duckbilled dinosaur that was so well preserved that even th skin had fossilized.

5. Scientists watched the birds care for their young.

6. Scientists found fossils of an animal sitting on eggs in a nest in Mongolia.

7. Scientists used medical scanners to see inside fossils of a dino skull. Inside the crest were hollow passages similar to the inside of a horn. Using computer simulations, they were able to recreate the sound made when air passed through the dinosaur's crest.

8. Scientists followed the footprints to the animal's burrow and then watched the animal care for its young.

9. Scientists can identify a general type of dinosaur from its footprints (tracks) but not the exact species.

10. In 2012, a scientist discovered fossilized footprints in a stream near Washington, DC.

Answers: 1) Biologist. 2) Paleontologist. 3) Paleontologist. 4) Paleontologist. 5) Biologist. 6) Paleontologist. 7) Paleontologist. 8) Biologist. 9) Paleontologist. 10) Paleontologist.

Body and Trace Fossils: Reading the Clues

Fossils are signs of things that have lived in the past. Fossils can be of plants or animals but all of the fossils mentioned in this book relate to dinosaurs.

Body fossils are physical proof of dinosaurs' existence. They are the body or body pieces (bones, claws, or teeth) of the actual dinosaur. In some cases, the body pieces turned into rock. In other cases, the bodies or body pieces were preserved in amber (fossilized tree resin).

Dinosaurs left traces: footprints, chew marks, nests, burrows, and even eggs. Sometimes those traces turned into fossils so that scientists can find them today. These trace fossils help scientists to learn about dinosaur behavior: what they ate, how they moved, and how they raised their young.

Paleontologists "read" the fossilized rock clues to learn about the dinosaurs. They use their knowledge of rocks (geology), living plants and animals (biology), and other science subjects to help them put together some of the puzzle pieces.

Several different fossilized nests and eggs have been found. One nest had 34 baby hatchlings with an adult nearby; all were sitting up with legs tucked underneath them. A nest found in Mongolia even had an adult male sitting on the eggs. Dinosaur's closest relatives, birds and crocodiles, also lay eggs and care for their young. Paleontologists can infer that at least some dinosaurs raised young the way birds and crocodiles do.

In 1999, a young teenager found a mummified dinosaur buried on his family farm in North Dakota. Scientists spent years digging the body out. The body was buried so quickly that the skin turned to stone, keeping its form and texture. The skin has geometric patterns, similar to a soccer ball. Using electron microscopes, scientists see that the skin had cell structures similar to modern-day birds and reptiles.

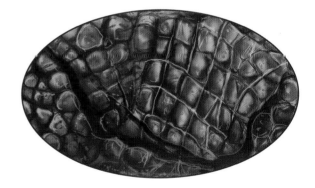

Some dinosaur fossils show a few feathers as impressions around the skeleton. Other dinosaur fossils show the dinosaurs were fully covered with feathers, much like today's birds. In 2011, scientists found several dinosaur feathers trapped in amber. The 78- to 79-million-year-old amber preserved the feathers in detail, including traces of their colors.

Bird feathers and human hair have tiny structures in their cells that carry color. The shape of the structure shows what color it is. For example, a round shape indicates a reddish color. Scientists can see the shapes under a powerful microscope and can infer that the dinosaur cell structures and colors would be similar to or the same as those today.

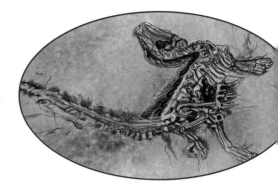

Fossilized poop is called coprolite. By studying it, scientists can tell what kinds of things the ancient animal had eaten. A coprolite thought to have come from a *Tyrannosaurus rex* (*T. rex*) has pieces of bone from a plant-eating dinosaur, confirming that *T. rex* were meat eaters.

Studying coprolites is not the only way that scientists can learn what dinosaurs ate. Some fossils have items in their stomachs. The bone of a pterosaur was found in the stomach of a Velociraptor. A duckbilled dinosaur's stomach had the remains of more than 40 kinds of plants! Fish scales and teeth were found in the stomach of a *Baryonyx walkeri*.

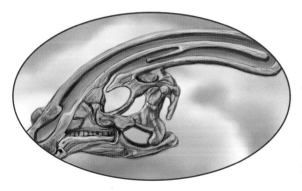

Parasaurolophus had a large bony crest on its head, but scientists didn't know what it was for. They used medical scanners to see inside the skull. The scientists found hollow passages similar to the inside of a horn. Using computer simulations, they recreated the sound made when air passed through the crest. Scientists think the dinos called to others over long distances similar to the way wolves and coyotes do.

"Sue" is the nickname of the largest and most complete *T. rex* skeleton ever found. Even though she was a fierce predator, her bones show evidence of a very hard life. Just like a doctor might see your broken bone with an x-ray, scientists can see that Sue had several broken bones in her ribs that had healed. Some scientists think this mighty predator may have died from an infection in her jaw.

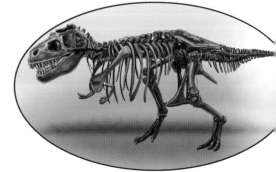

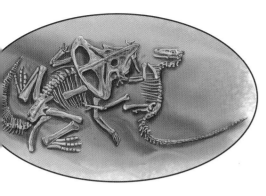

Just as wild animals may fight for survival today, dinosaurs fought too. Two fighting dinosaurs, a *Velociraptor* and a *Protoceratops*, must have been caught in a collapsing sand dune in what is now Mongolia. The collapsing sand buried them so quickly that their bodies were fossilized.

iscovered in China in 2004, the *Mei long* fossil is of sleeping feathered dinosaur. Scientists think it was uried by volcanic ash or died by poisonous gas from volcanic eruption. The dinosaur was sleeping with its et tucked under its body and its head under a wing— ist as many birds sleep today. The dinosaur would ave been about the size of a duck.

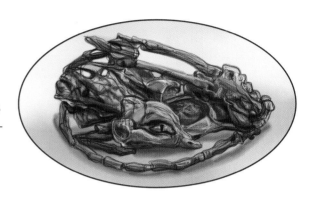

Just as you might leave footprints in mud, so did the dinosaurs. Sometimes these footprints, or tracks, fossilized so that we can see them today. Many tracks together make a trackway. These tracks and trackways help tell us how large the dinosaurs were, whether the dinosaurs were walking, running, slipping in the mud, or even swimming! The shape of the prints also tells us whether the track maker ate plants or meat.

udying the skulls of *Pachycephalosaurus yomingensis* ("thick-headed lizard"), scientists found gns of injury. They can't say for sure, but think ead butting may have caused the injuries. Since ale bighorn sheep head butt to see who will get the males, scientists infer that the dinosaurs probably d the same.

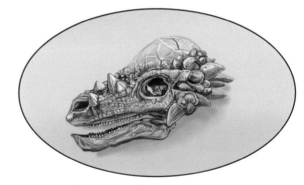

Most scientists agree that birds are living dinosaurs. Birds are the only present-day animals that have feathers and hollow bones. Many scientists are most excited about the way that birds still stand and run on the balls of their three-toed feet. Just like many dinosaurs, all birds have long and mobile S-shaped necks. Scientists were able to remove the remains of proteins from a *T. rex* fossil. The proteins were most similar to the proteins of an ostrich and a chicken.

Thanks to the following scientists for verifying the information in this book:
- Dr. Phil Bell, Vertebrate Paleontologist, University of New England, Australia
- Dr. Karen Chin, Curator of Paleontology, Museum of Natural History and Associate Professor of Geological Sciences at University of Colorad
- Dr. Jacques Gauthier, Professor of Geology, Yale University and Curator of Vertebrate Paleontology at the Peabody Museum
- Dr. Tyler Lyson, Marmarth Research Foundation and Researcher for the Smithsonian Institution National Museum of Natural Histor
- Dr. Ryan McKellar, Invertebrate Paleontologist, Postdoctoral Fellow, University of Alberta
- Dr. Joseph Peterson, Vertebrate Paleontologist, Assistant Professor of Geology, University of Wisconsin—Oshkosh
- William F. Simpson, McCarter Collections Manager, Fossil Vertebrates, Field Museum of Natural History
- Dr. David Varricchio, Associate Professor of Paleontology, Montana State University
- Dr. Thomas E. Williamson, Curator of Paleontology, New Mexico Museum of Natural History and Science

Library of Congress Cataloging-in-Publication Data

Donald, Rhonda Lucas, 1962- author.
 Dino treasures / by Rhonda Lucas Donald ; illustrated by Cathy Morrison.
    pages cm
Audience: Ages 4-8.
 Audience: K to grade 3.
 ISBN 978-1-62855-450-2 (English hardcover) -- ISBN 978-1-62855-458-8 (English pbk.) -- ISBN (invalid) 978-1-62855-474-8 (English downloadable ebook) -- ISBN 978-1-62855-490-8 (English interactive dual-language ebook) -- ISBN 978-1-62855-466-3 (Spanish pbk.) -- ISBN 978-1-62855-482-3 (Spanish downloadable ebook) -- ISBN 978-1-62855-498-4 (Spanish interactive dual-language ebook)
1. Dinosaurs--Juvenile literature. 2. Fossils--Juvenile literature. 3. Paleontologists--Juvenile literature. I. Morrison, Cathy, illustrator. II. Title.
 QE861.5.D68 2014
 567.9--dc23

2014009961

Translated into Spanish: Dino tesoros
Lexile® Level: 660   key phrases for educators: dinosaurs, fossils, scientists/jobs

Bibliography:
"Birds are Dinosaurs." *American Museum of Natural History*. Accessed March 20, 2014. http://www.amnh.org/explore/science-topics/
    birds-are-dinosaurs.
"Cretaceous Footprints Found at Goddard." August 23, 2012. *NASA*. http://www.nasa.gov/centers/goddard/news/features/2012/nodosaur.html
"The Fighting Dinosaurs." *American Museum of Natural History*. Accessed March 20, 2014. http://www.amnh.org/exhibitions/past-
    exhibitions/fighting-dinos/the-fighting-dinosaurs.
Hopkin, Michael. "Fossil Dinosaur Slept Like a Bird." October 13, 2004. *Nature*. Accessed March 20, 2014. http://www.nature.com/
    news/2004/041011/full/news041011-7.html
"How Did Dinosaurs Behave?" *Smithsonian National Museum of Natural History*. Accessed March 20, 2014. http://www.mnh.si.edu/
    exhibits/backyard-dinosaurs/how-did-dinosaurs-behave.cfm.
"How Do Scientists Know What Dinosaurs Ate Without Looking at Their Teeth? *University of California, Santa Barbara*. Accessed March
    20, 2014. http://scienceline.ucsb.edu/getkey.php?key=198.
Joyce, Christopher. "Dinosaur Dads Cared for Young, Researchers Say." December 19, 2008. *NPR*. Accessed March 20, 2014. http://www
    npr.org/templates/story/story.php?storyId=98442140
Joyce, Christopher. "Fossil Hunters Uncover Rare Dinosaur Skin." July 3, 2009. *NPR*. Accessed March 20, 2014. http://www.npr.org/
    templates/story/story.php?storyId=106229723.
Markey, Sean. "Dino Dung: Paleontology's Next Frontier?" March 12, 2003. *National Geographic News*. Accessed March 20, 2014. http://
    news.nationalgeographic.com/news/2003/03/0312_030312_dinodung.html
Sloan, Chris. "Dinosaur True Colors Revealed for First Time." January 27, 2010. *National Geographic Daily News*. Accessed March 20, 201
    http://news.nationalgeographic.com/news/2010/01/100127-dinosaur-feathers-colors-nature/
Switek, Brian. "Fossil Testifies to Pachycephalosaur Pain." May 3, 2012. *Smithsonian.com*. Accessed March 20, 2014. http://www.
    smithsonianmag.com/science-nature/fossil-testifies-to-pachycephalosaur-pain-79971905/
Switek, Brian. "How Parasaurolophus Set the Mood." February 14, 2011. *Smithsonian.com*. Accessed March 20, 2014. http://www.
    smithsonianmag.com/science-nature/how-parasaurolophus-set-the-mood-94657740/?no-ist=
"SUE's Injuries and Illnesses." SUE at *The Field Museum*. Accessed March 20, 2014. http://archive.fieldmuseum.org/sue/#photo-gallery-
    special-features-3.
Trinity-Stevens, Annette. "Sept. 9 paper with MSU coauthor underscores dinosaur parenting." *Montana State University*. Accessed March
    20, 2014. http://www.montana.edu/cpa/news/nwview.php?article=1886.
Wilford, John Noble. "Feathers Trapped in Amber Reveal a More Colorful Dinosaur Age." September 15, 2011. *The New York Times*.
    Accessed March 20, 2014. http://www.nytimes.com/2011/09/20/science/20feather.html?_r=1&

Manufactured in China, November, 20
This product conforms to CPSIA 20
First Printi

Arbordale Publishi
Mt. Pleasant, SC 294
www.ArbordalePublishing.c